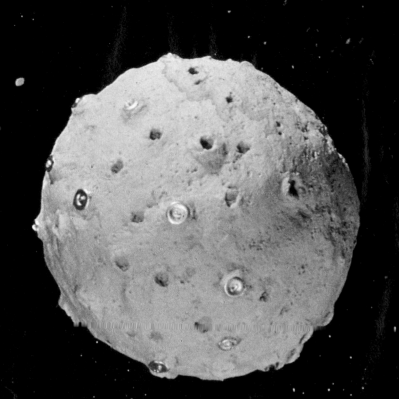

A *Little, Brown* Book

First published in Great Britain in 1993
by Little, Brown and Company

Copyright © Text Oliver Postgate 1993
Copyright © Illustrations Peter Firmin 1993

A CIP catalogue record for this book is available from
the British Library.

ISBN 0 316 90535 6

Printed and bound in Italy by Graphicom SRL

Little, Brown and Company (UK) Limited
165 Great Dover Street
London SE1 4YA

Clangers

The Sky-moos

STORY BY OLIVER POSTGATE
PICTURES BY PETER FIRMIN

LITTLE, BROWN AND COMPANY

Small Clanger was sitting beside the music trees looking away across the curved surface of the little moon which was the Clangers' world.

Apart from the metal lids of the cave-holes there was very little to look at. Nothing was growing there.

The landscape was blue and bare and lumpy, except for the one cloud that was floating a little way away. Small Clanger wondered whether the cloud ever got bored, having nothing to do except float.

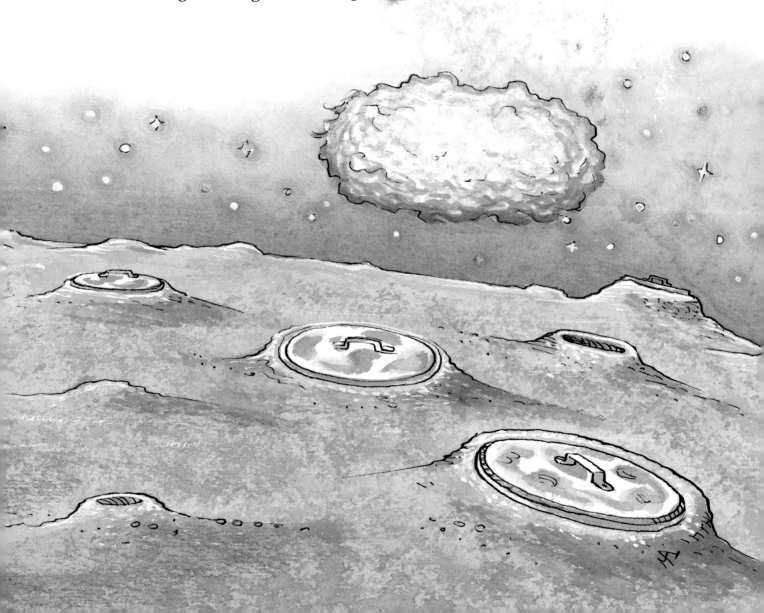

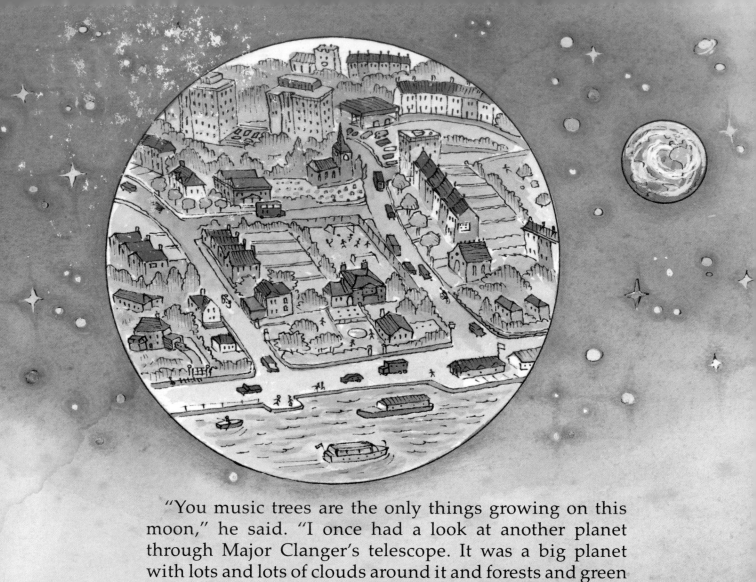

"You music trees are the only things growing on this moon," he said. "I once had a look at another planet through Major Clanger's telescope. It was a big planet with lots and lots of clouds around it and forests and green trees and houses and gardens and people running about. People are walking creatures like Clangers, but they are ever so thin and have to wear lots of clothes to keep warm. They aren't as clever as Clangers but they do have lovely gardens."

He sighed. "I wish we could have gardens here. I think this planet is *boring*! There is nothing to look at and nothing ever happens!"

That was rather a silly thing to say because, as you know, once you say something like, "Nothing ever happens," something usually does happen, quite soon, and it isn't always something you like.

From somewhere high in the sky Small Clanger heard faint music. It wasn't the *pling-plang* sort of sound the music trees make. This was a soft sound, like a running stream or a flute being played very gently.

Small Clanger looked up and saw, floating slowly across the sky, a delicate circular thing, made up of a web of fine threads, with a tiny black dot at the centre.

The thing, whatever it was, floated slowly around the Clangers' moon. Small Clanger followed it and watched as it floated closer and closer until it landed lightly on the ground. Then he ran forward and grabbed it. The circle of fine threads crumpled away, leaving only the hard black knob. Small Clanger put a stone on top of it and ran indoors.

"Quick, Tiny!" he shouted. "Something has fallen from the sky!"

"What is it?"

"I don't know. Come and look!"

They ran back to look at the thing and saw that something had happened to it. The black knob had split open and from inside it a green shoot was growing. The Clangers watched the shoot grow and grow. Then, when it was nearly as tall as a Clanger, it suddenly stopped growing and began to wilt.

Tiny Clanger knew what was wrong. She stood on a hill and whistled to the cloud. "Come here! Come here Cloud! This shoot needs watering."

The cloud knew exactly what to do. It hovered over the shoot and rained lots of bright raindrops on it.

The effect was marvellous. The shoot straightened up and began to grow again. Soon it grew branches, and leaves sprouted from them. Then, last of all, it grew a crown of perfect red and white flowers.

All the Clangers came out to admire the beautiful plant.

"If we had lots of those we could have a proper garden," said Small Clanger.

"The cloud did it," said Tiny Clanger. "The cloud rained on the shoot and it grew. The cloud is clever."

The cloud was very pleased to be called clever and its raindrops rang like bells.

"The cloud is pretty as well as clever," said Tiny Clanger, and she picked flowers from the new plant and stuck them all over the outside of the cloud.

The cloud was very pleased to be so pretty and it sailed backwards and forwards across the sky, showing off its jacket of red and white flowers.

Then the petals began to fall from the flowers. The seed-pods fattened and grew rings of fine threads like thistledown and, last of all, the rings floated away from the cloud and began to fall to the ground, just like the first one that Small Clanger had seen. The delighted cloud sailed over them, raining bright raindrops on them as they floated down.

"Now we shall have a proper garden," said Small Clanger.

"We might have too much garden," suggested Mother Clanger, beginning to feel a bit worried.

Mother Clanger was quite right to be worried because the seeds sprouted at once and an army of green shoots sprang up out of the ground. They grew tall, with branches and leaves and more flowers. The flowers fell and more seeds floated away. In no time at all the Clangers' planet had changed from an empty place into a garden and then from a garden into a forest and then from a forest into a jungle.

The Clangers backed away from the wall of bright greenery as it grew all around them. They backed away right around their world until they met the wall of greenery coming around the other way! Then there was only one thing to do.

Major Clanger opened the last metal lid and they all dived into the caves. Then, before any seeds could float in after them, Major Clanger clanged the lid shut.

"Phew!" he said. "That was a near thing!"

"Won't it be marvellous to have such a lovely garden?" said Small Clanger.

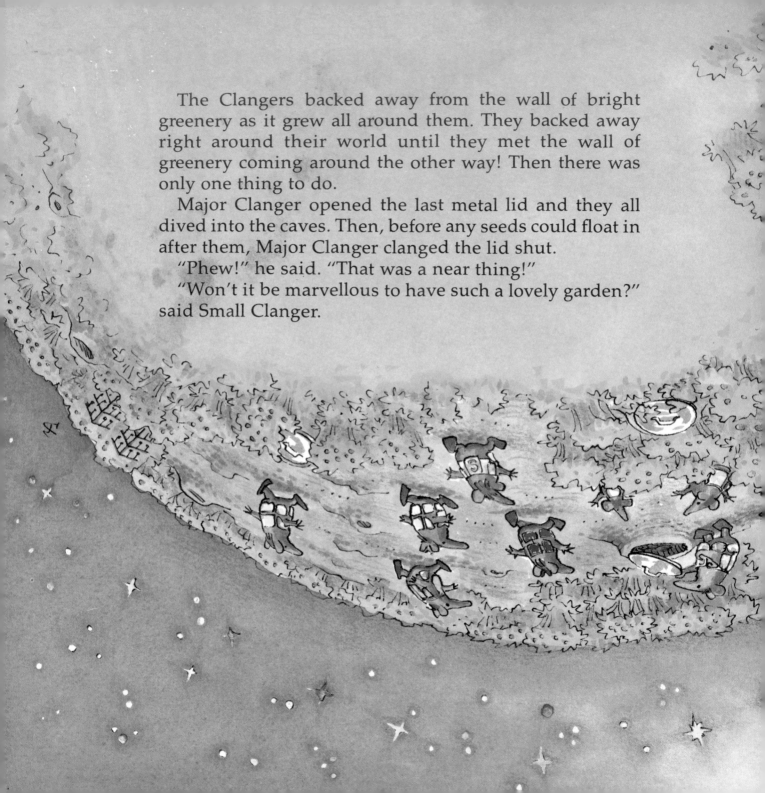

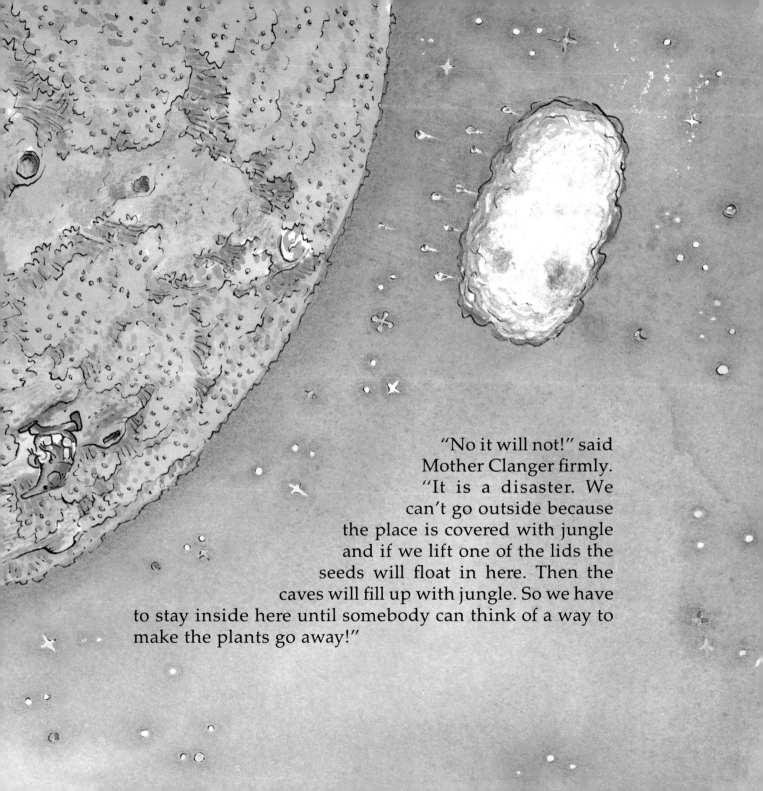

"No it will not!" said
Mother Clanger firmly.
"It is a disaster. We
can't go outside because
the place is covered with jungle
and if we lift one of the lids the
seeds will float in here. Then the
caves will fill up with jungle. So we have
to stay inside here until somebody can think of a way to
make the plants go away!"

"Oh dear," said Small Clanger. "I didn't think of that."
None of the Clangers could think of a way to make the plants go away.

"I wish there was somebody we could ask," said Mother Clanger sadly, "but nobody can see us in here."

"I could send up a sky-rocket which would burst with blue and white stars," suggested Major Clanger, "but I don't expect there is anybody out there to see it."

"Yes there is!" shouted Tiny Clanger. She ran to fetch the radio hat that the Iron Chicken had given her.

Beep-beep, it went.

Over the radio Tiny told her friend the Iron Chicken exactly what had happened.

"No trouble at all," said the Iron Chicken cheerfully. "This is a job for the sky-moos. They will enjoy it. You set up the rocket while I send a radio message to the sky-moos. Then, when I send you a beep, you set off the rocket and the sky-moos will see it. Over and out."

And that is exactly what they did.
Beep-beep, went Tiny's radio hat.
Major Clanger opened a lid.
"Fire the rocket!" he shouted.
WHOOOOOOSH! Away went the rocket.
Clatter-clatter, bang, bang, bang . . .
The blue and white stars burst from
it and filled the sky with light.

Clang! Major Clanger slammed down the
lid, just in time – three of the seeds had tried
to float in!

Then the Clangers sat in their caves and
waited for the sky-moos to arrive.

If you have done a lot of travelling in space you will of course know what a sky-moo looks like. It is a very large, very beautiful beast. It is a bit like a hippopotamus but it has tiny horns and absolutely enormous ears which, as no doubt you have guessed, it uses as wings. Sky-moos are very good at flying but they are even better at something else – eating! These kindly creatures love to eat lots and lots of greenery, leaves, stalks, flowers – they chomp them up like you eat your tea and Clangers eat blue-string pudding.

"Here they come!" whispered Tiny Clanger.

Crouched under the lids the Clangers heard the *zoom* . . . *zoom* . . . *zoom* . . . of the sky-moos' great ear-wings as they flew in. Then they heard the *bump* . . . *bump* . . . *bump* . . . as they landed. Then at last they heard the *scrunch* . . . *scrunch* . . . *munch* . . . *gulp*.

"They are eating!" whistled Tiny Clanger.

"Hooray! Hooray! the sky-moos are eating!" whistled the Clangers.

The sky-moos munched and scrunched and chomped and swallowed and munched again, working their way methodically around the planet, eating up every shred of greenery in their path.

"The sky-moos will be thirsty after their dinner," said Mother Clanger. "We must ask the Soup Dragon to give us some green soup for them."

So the Clangers took every mug, bowl and pudding-pan they could find and went to the soup wells.

The Soup Dragon gave them all the green soup they wanted and the Clangers pushed open the big doors of the main cave and stepped out. There was hardly a stalk of greenery anywhere to be seen. But there were several sky-moos.

"Soup! Soup for you!" whistled the Clangers.

"Oooooooh," mooed the sky-moos, "Oooooooh . . . look! . . . soooooup."

The thirsty sky-moos gathered round. They dipped their huge snouts into the bowls and pudding-pans and slurped up great quantities of green soup.

"Oooooh . . . that's gooood . . . goood soooooup!"

They turned slowly around and began to beat their ear-wings . . . "Goooooodbye . . . goodbye . . ."

The sound of slurping and mooing was mixed with the *zooom* . . . *zooom* . . . of the sky-moos' great ear-wings as, one by one, they lifted off and headed, feeling well fed and happy, back towards their own distant planet.

"Goodbye! Goodbye sky-moos! Thankyou!" whistled the Clangers.

Small Clanger looked at the empty blue landscape of their moon. "I think I prefer it without a garden," he said.